A NOTE ABOUT THE STORY

"Romantic ideas remembered from childhood storybooks and revived by real-life events can be powerful creative forces," Pam Newton writes. When she lived in Izmir, Turkey, with her husband, she awakened one morning to the distant, plodding dong-dong-dong of brass bells as a camel caravan passed by her window. The evocative and magical sound drew her to the window and she marveled at the sight. Where had they come from? she wondered. Where were they going? And what treasures did they carry? Suddenly she was transported into the realm of remembered story-book fantasies.

Many years passed, but Pam never forgot that caravan and the many others she saw during her year in Turkey. When she came upon "The Stonecutter," she saw a way to bring her experience to life, and she began to work on her own version of the story.

She found several versions with Japanese and Chinese settings, but an Indian version was the most visually exciting to her. Fond of Persian minia-tures and especially partial to Indian Mughal paintings, she felt she had just the right setting and reference for her story.

By combining elements from the various stonecutter tales she had found with her own artistic vision, she has created a colorful, vibrant story with authentic details. At last, her "dear old caravan idea" has found a home.

—*Tomie dePaola, Creative Director*
WHITEBIRD BOOKS

The STONECUTTER

AN INDIAN FOLKTALE RETOLD AND ILLUSTRATED BY

Pam Newton

A WHITEBIRD BOOK
G. P. Putnam's Sons
New York

G.P. Putnam's Sons, a division of
The Putnam & Grosset Group
200 Madison Avenue, New York, NY 10016
Published simultaneously in Canada.
Printed in Hong Kong by South China Printing Co. (1988) Ltd.
Type design by Gunta Alexander
Library of Congress Cataloging-in-Publication Data
Newton, Patricia Montgomery
The stonecutter: an Indian folktale/retold and illustrated
by Patricia M. Newton.   p.   cm.   "A Whitebird book."
Summary: A retelling of a traditional Indian tale in which
a discontented stonecutter is never satisfied with each wish
that is granted him.
[1. Folklore—India.] I. Title. PZ8.1.N48St 1990
398.21'09561—dc20 [E] 89-32920 CIP AC
ISBN 0-399-22187-5
1 3 5 7 9 10 8 6 4 2
First impression

For Zachary

Once there was a poor stonecutter who lived in a small hut in the forest on the side of a mountain.

Every morning while the sun was still a yellow ribbon of promise in the eastern sky, the stonecutter picked up his tools and climbed the mountain path until he arrived at a big rock in the side of the mountain. Along the way trees waved morning greetings and calling birds soared across the mountainside. A tiger, hidden in his cave, yawned and curled up for a nap.

Before the stonecutter began to work he prayed to the mountain spirit for blessing and protection. Then he hammered and chipped and smoothed and polished the building blocks he made from the stones he took out of the mountain.

Although he worked hard and his days were long, he never minded until the day he delivered some blocks of stone to repair a wall at the home of a rich man. The stonecutter had never seen such splendor. He looked at the luxury surrounding him and marveled. From then on, the stonecutter spent his days wishing for comfort and his nights dreaming of wealth.

It grew harder and harder to be a poor stonecutter. Every morning he climbed the mountain path on feet heavy as stones. One day as he neared the big rock he threw down his tools and prayed to the mountain spirit. But this time he cried out for more. His angry demands and cries of discontent shook the forest, scattering the birds into the air. The sleeping tiger, hidden in his cave, rolled over and opened one great golden eye.

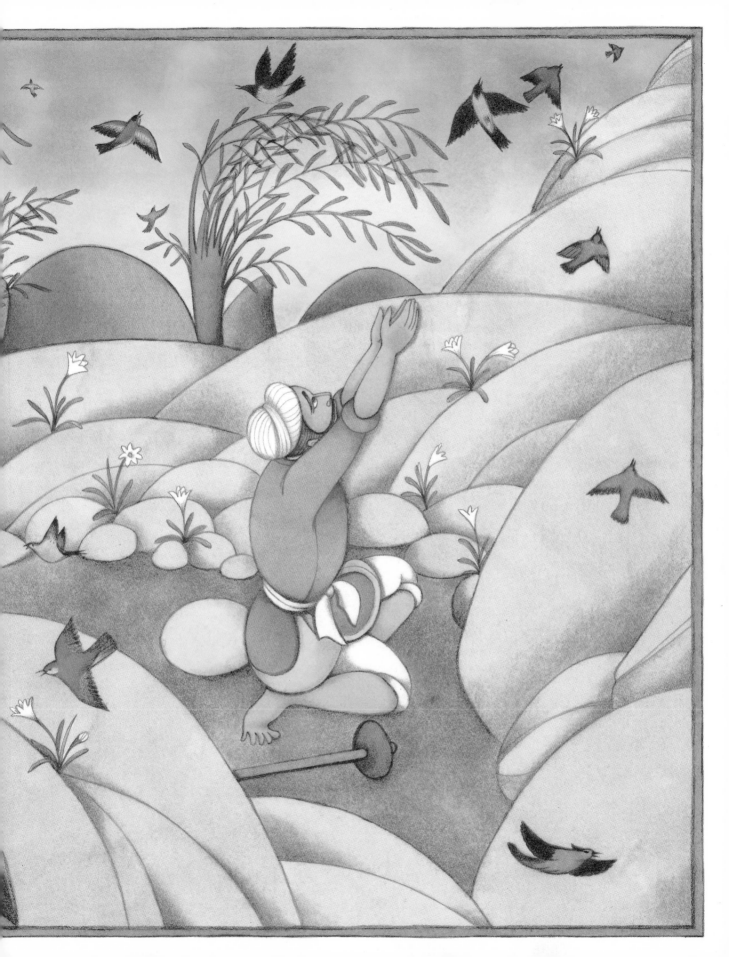

Deep within the mountain the spirit heard the stonecutter's cries and decided to grant his prayers.

The spirit stilled the trees and calmed the birds and soothed the tiger back to sleep. The stonecutter's heart was filled with hope so that when he raised his hammer and began to work, he believed his prayers would soon be answered.

The next day, as he walked to the city to deliver some blocks of stone, the stonecutter saw a merchant leading camels heaped high with silks and spices for the market. He stood by the side of the road and watched.

"A stonecutter is nothing compared to a rich merchant," he said, sighing, and squeezed his eyes shut against the dust.

"If only I were a rich merchant," he cried, as he covered his ears to keep out the shouts of the camel drivers. "Then I could be truly happy."

Far away inside the mountain, the spirit heard his wish and made it true.

When the stonecutter opened his eyes, his blocks of stone had disappeared and in their place stood all the wealth of a merchant. He bowed his richly turbaned head and murmured his gratitude. Surrounded by his new wealth, he began his journey to the city to sell his goods.

But even a wealthy merchant grows tired and thirsty traveling a long, hot road in the middle of the day.

"I will stop there for rest and refreshment," the stonecutter said to his camel drivers, pointing at a distant bright-flowered hill.

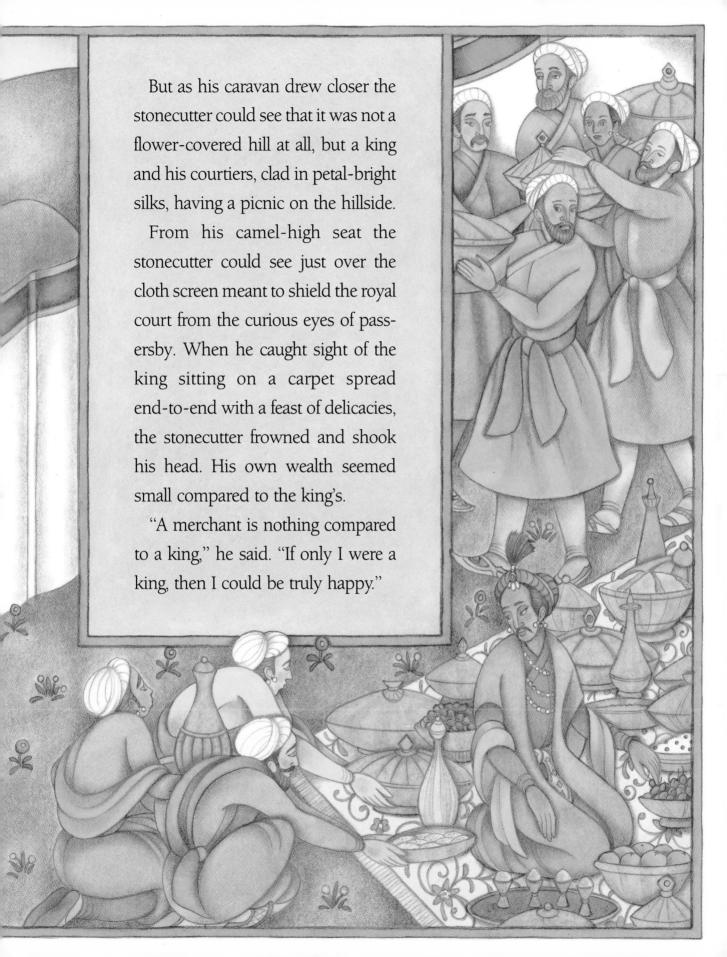

But as his caravan drew closer the stonecutter could see that it was not a flower-covered hill at all, but a king and his courtiers, clad in petal-bright silks, having a picnic on the hillside.

From his camel-high seat the stonecutter could see just over the cloth screen meant to shield the royal court from the curious eyes of pass-ersby. When he caught sight of the king sitting on a carpet spread end-to-end with a feast of delicacies, the stonecutter frowned and shook his head. His own wealth seemed small compared to the king's.

"A merchant is nothing compared to a king," he said. "If only I were a king, then I could be truly happy."

The words were barely spoken when—wonder of wonders—the stonecutter became a king!

A servant offered him a tray of sherbets. The sweet pink ices cooled his dry throat. Perfumed courtiers hovered like butterflies, filling the air with the scent of roses and sandalwood. The stonecutter kicked off his slippers and settled into his cushions, nibbling first from one tray of delights and then another.

Though his every desire was fulfilled, the afternoon sun burned down on the hillside and the stonecutter began to feel hot. His beard glistened with sweat and his skin blistered and itched.

Shielding his eyes with his hand, the stonecutter tried to look heavenward. High above, the sun blazed powerful and brilliant, too great for even a king to gaze upon.

"I was wrong," moaned the stonecutter, wiping his brow with a silk scarf. "A king is nothing compared to the sun. If only I were the sun, then I could be truly happy."

His wish spoken, the stonecutter at once became the scorching sun, whirling red-hot across the heavens, and dazzling the world with his fiery strength.

"Now there is nothing more glorious than I am," he declared, seeing each flower's face turn to him and every tree reach up, up to embrace him.

"Even a powerful king cannot stop me from burning his skin," declared the stonecutter, as his thousand wheeling arms searched the earth for a king.

Just then a small cloud drifted across the sky and passed between the sun and the earth. The stonecutter cried out, for his face was hidden from the earth.

He was utterly powerless.

"I was wrong," he groaned. "The sun is nothing compared to a cloud. If only I were a cloud, then I could be truly happy."

And so saying, the stonecutter was transformed into a pale gossamer cloud, with the sun scowling at his back, the earth spread below, and the sky all around. He had nothing better in the world to do but float along effortlessly, puffed up with the pride and power of his new position.

But not for long.

As quickly as the cloud had covered the sun, a wind arrived and swept the cloud away.

"Oh-h-h," sobbed the stonecutter, as the wind's icy breath tore him apart. "A cloud is nothing compared to the wind. If only I were the wind, then I could be truly happy."

At once the stonecutter became the wind, tossing the clouds across the sky as he rushed to earth.

"Whee-e-e-e!" He blew over the ocean making waves.

"Whir-r-r-r!" He rolled across the fields, bending flowers and grasses.

"Who-o-o-sh!" He rustled through the trees, snapping branches.

Everywhere the stonecutter went he made a great commotion until he met a mountain. Although he blustered and raged and blew he could not move it. Not even a little.

"The wind is nothing compared to a mountain," huffed the stonecutter. "If only I were a mountain, then I could be truly happy."

"Now," boasted the stonecutter as once again his wish was granted, "a wind cannot move me."

"A cloud cannot cover me."

"The sun cannot burn me."

"A king cannot equal my majesty."

"And surely a merchant is nothing compared to a mountain."

But as he spoke, a man climbed up the side of the mountain. He carried a hammer, and when he began to pound, pound, pound, the stonecutter cried out: "I am the mountain and there is nothing on earth or in the heavens as powerful as I am."

The man continued to hammer and chip and smooth and polish, making building blocks from the stones he took out of the mountain.

"Oh-h-h, no-o-o," wailed the stonecutter. "I was wrong."

"Stone by stone, even a mountain is nothing compared to a stonecutter. If only I were a stonecutter, then I would be truly happy."

His wish spoken, he found himself standing on the side of the mountain. He was a stonecutter once again.

As he climbed his well-worn path, trees waved and birds soared and sang. The tiger slumbered in his cave.

The stonecutter offered a prayer of thanks to the mountain spirit. A feeling of contentment settled over him.

"At last I am happy to be a stonecutter—truly happy."

Then he began to hammer and chip and smooth and polish, making building blocks from the stones he took out of the mountain.